RAVEN
returns the
WATER

Anne Cameron

HARBOUR PUBLISHING CO. LTD.
1987

Text © Anne Cameron 1987
Illustrations © Nelle Olsen 1987
Cover and book design by Gaye Hammond
ISBN 0-920080-19-7

Harbour Publishing Co. Ltd.
Box 219, Madeira Park, B.C.
Canada V0N 2H0

Printed in Canada by Friesen Printers

Canadian Cataloguing in Publication Data

Cameron, Anne, 1938 —
    Raven returns the water

    ISBN 0-920080-19-7

    1. Indians of North America — Northwest Coast of North
America — Legends — Juvenile literature. I. Title.
PS8555.A43R3 1987   j398.2'08997-795   C87-091138-4
PZ8.1.C35Ra 1987

When I was growing up on Vancouver Island I met a woman who was a storyteller. She shared many stories with me, and later, gave me permission to share them with others.

This woman's name was KLOPINUM. In English her name means "Keeper of the River of Copper." It is to her this book is dedicated, and it is in the spirit of sharing, which she taught me, these stories are offered to all small children. I hope you will enjoy them as much as I did.

Anne Cameron

There came a time when the water began to disappear. The rain fell less often, and when it fell there was less of it, and soon the lakes began to shrink, the rivers began to dwindle in size, and the ocean receded from the shore.

The people had to save their water and use it only for drinking. They had to eat their food raw, for there was not enough water for boiling and steaming. They stopped bathing, and guarded their drinking water carefully.

With no water for bathing, there was no water for purification ceremonies, and without purification ceremonies, the hunters could not hunt, the fishers could not fish, and the newborn could not be welcomed to this life.

The animals suffered and began to die of thirst. The fish had no water in which to make their homes, and the plants wilted. Even the huge trees began to die for lack of water.

Raven was so thirsty she thought she would die. She flew to the creek and found it dry. She flew to the river and found it dry. She flew to the lake and found it dry.

She knew she had to do something.

She knew she had to find the water or the entire world would die.

She put a round, smooth pebble under her tongue to make the saliva flow, and swallowed her own saliva. Then, only slightly refreshed, she flew in search of the missing water.

She flew over high mountains and saw that the snow and ice which usually sits on the tops of the mountains had melted and vanished. She flew over deep valleys and saw that the mighty rivers usually found in the hearts of the valleys had dried. Only rocks and sand showed where the rivers had been. She flew over huge bare patches which had once been lakes.

She saw plains and prairies covered with rocks and dirt, with sand and gravel. She saw fields that once blossomed with flowers and grass, and were now barren and dry. She saw forests where the trees were no longer green but dried brown, pointing like arrows to the sky, their bark peeling, their limbs bare.

9

She flew until even her powerful wings began to ache. And one evening, just as the sun began to dip behind the mountains in the land from which Raven had come, she saw some small lights twinkling in the distance.

Raven went to investigate and found the last green valley on earth. The last place where there were trees and flowers and grass and birds and butterflies and hummingbirds and all things beautiful and precious.

11

And in the middle of the valley, sound asleep, a giant frog, her belly swollen and distended. The bright lights Raven had noticed were drops of water which had fallen from the giant frog's mouth. They lay glittering in the last light of the setting sun.

Raven tiptoed quietly to the giant frog and sipped the water which had fallen from the frog's mouth.

Cool, refreshing water! Raven knew she had never tasted anything so delicious in her life! She took another drink and the frog opened her eye.

"That is MY water you are drinking," the frog croaked, and she lashed out with her long sticky tongue, meaning to knock Raven away from the water.

Raven hopped quickly and avoided the tongue of the frog. She drank another drop of water, her head cocked to one side, watching the frog to see what she would do. Frog lashed with her tongue again, and again Raven hopped out of the way.

"It is NOT your water," Raven contradicted. "Water belongs to everybody and everything."

"It's mine," Frog argued, slickering out her tongue and scooping up some of the spilled drops.

"Water belongs to the trees, too," Raven said firmly. "And to the flowers who will die without it."

"It's mine, all mine," Frog insisted, and slithered out her tongue for more.

"Water belongs to the fish and to the animals and to the people and to itself," Raven replied. "No one person or thing has the right to keep the water, for water is life, and without clean water, nothing can live."

But Frog wasn't going to listen to reason. She lay there, so full of water she couldn't move, so full of water her skin was stretched tighter than any drumskin, trying to capture and gulp for herself those last precious drops.

Raven knew force was not the answer. Raven knew fighting would not solve the problem. Even if Raven managed to beat Frog and made her give back the water, there would come another day and Frog would again steal the water. Raven knew no matter how many times she beat Frog, unless Frog learned to respect the water, and share it, and live in harmony again, there would be no peace or security or safety, and there would be other times of drought.

As Frog flicked out her tongue and lapped up another drop of water, Raven dropped the little stone she had kept under her tongue.

The stone landed on Frog's tongue, and Frog pulled the stone into her mouth and swallowed it.

Raven waited.

Frog blinked her big round eye.

Her belly quivered.

The expression of Frog's face became one of sadness.

"Oh," Frog croaked. "Oh my!"

"What's wrong?" asked Raven, sounding very kind and very concerned.

"My stomach hurts," Frog admitted.

"I think," Raven said gently, "you have overextended yourself. I think," she said softly, "you have swallowed a rock."

"I have a bellyache," Frog moaned.

Raven waited.

Soon a large tear escaped from Frog's eye.

"See," Raven said reasonably, "your body can't hold all that water AND that rock. You have to give up one or the other or you'll never get rid of that bellyache."

"Take the rock," Frog bargained, "because it's MY water and I want it all."

Raven did nothing.

"Well," Frog demanded, her face twisted in pain. "Are you going to help me or not?"

"Probably not," Raven shrugged.

Frog stared at Raven and another tear escaped her. "Why not?" she asked pathetically. "Can't you see I'm in agony?"

"Guess that's what you get for being greedy," Raven agreed, although, as we all know, Raven herself is a glutton.

"Please?" Frog begged.

"What if some of your water spills?" Raven asked. "Are you going to get angry with me and try to slap me with that long tongue of yours?"

"No," Frog promised. "I will keep my mouth shut and tongue wrapped up inside me, and I won't do anything at all to hurt you. I promise."

So Raven poked Frog in the belly. Then poked again, harder. A gush of water came from Frog's mouth, landed on the ground, and flowed away, becoming a small river.

"I have to find out where that rock is," Raven explained. "I'm not poking at you just because I like to hurt you. I have to be very sure where that rock is." And she poked again and again, and each time, Frog winced, and water gushed from her mouth.

The small river grew into a bigger river and flowed out of the valley to the parched land beyond. The thirsty earth soaked it up gratefully. Flowers drank it through their roots, the grass began to live again, and the fish, which had almost died, were saved.

"I think I've found it," Raven said.

"Oh, I feel so sick," Frog moaned. "Please remove that rock."

Raven jabbed her powerful beak and pierced the side of the frog. The water that had been trapped inside gushed through the hole.

"Oh, I haven't felt this good in months!" Frog smiled. "It feels so much better to be in the water than to have the water in me."

"Remember that," Raven laughed. And to help Frog remember, she left the rock where Frog could see it.

Raven rolled the escaping water up like a dance cape, and tucked it under her wing.

"Thank you," said Frog, shrinking steadily as the water escaped from inside her.

"Thank you," said Raven, flying off with the water tucked under her wing.

Raven flew home, and, as she flew, drops fell from the blanket of water and refilled the lakes. Raven poured water into the streams and creeks, the ponds and rivers. She poured water back into the ocean, and the oolichan, herring, cod, salmon, and halibut were saved.

Mussels, clams, oysters, and crabs celebrated the return of the water.

Mink, otter, seal, sea lions, and walrus danced with joy.

All the plants and animals were saved, and when the green leaves again appeared on the alder, maple, and birch, Raven knew the world was safe.

She sat high in the branches of a tree and sent her sharp call to the skies to tell the clouds they, too, would soon be filled with water.

When Frog heard the sound of Raven's cry, she realized what she had almost done, and she felt sorry for her greediness. She swam to the rock Raven had removed from her belly, and Frog climbed up on the rock. She croaked "sor-ry, sor-ry," and all of creation forgave her.

And to this day, if you move carefully and quietly, you may see Frog sitting on a rock on the bank of a pond or lake, or in a quiet stream or river, her throat swelling with the promise that she will never again take all the water.

And Raven calls to her often as she flies overhead. "Rock," she calls, and if you listen carefully, you will hear her.